Ghost School

Adam Guillain

Illustrated by Bill Ledger

It was Monday night. Stanley was doing his maths homework. His mum was lying on the sofa reading his school report, and his dad was doing the ironing.

"It's quite clear to me that the teachers at Stanley's school don't push him," said Mum.

"Well, what's he good at?" asked Dad. He pressed the iron down onto his trousers.

Stanley's mum read the report again.

"He's average at most things, but brilliant at ... " she paused and shook her head, " ... nothing. I don't think they notice him because he's so quiet and well-behaved."

"But Stanley must have a talent for something," said Dad, admiring his ironed trousers. "Maybe Stanley needs a school with a bit more spirit!"

He grabbed a pair of crumpled underpants and squirted them with water.

"We need to find a school that will bring out his hidden talents," Dad said.

"Perhaps he could go and visit Aunt Mabel," said Mum.

Suddenly, a big cloud of steam burst from the iron. Stanley looked up from his homework. For a moment, his dad appeared to vanish.

"Dad?" he called.

Slowly, the haze lifted. Just the mention of Aunt Mabel had turned Stanley's dad white.

"Whoooo," Stanley moaned. He pulled his white T-shirt over his face and wiggled his fingers like a ghost. "That was spooky."

"You mean Aunt Mabel who worked as a cook on Rutland Moor? In that old, crumbling mansion in the middle of nowhere?" his dad trembled. He put the iron down onto his underpants and stared blankly at the wall.

"It's a school, not a ruin," replied Mum, getting excited. "The building is being restored."

Stanley's dad didn't even blink.

"Aunt Mabel wrote only last week," Mum went on. "She says the new teachers are great. Perhaps *they* could unlock Stanley's hidden talents."

Stanley could smell something burning.

"I thought Aunt Mabel died in a bus crash," said Dad, sniffing.

Stanley's mum looked uneasy. "It was a mistake," she whispered. "There wasn't a crash at all. She's fine. You know how much fun she used to be."

"I remember she was a bit bonkers," said Dad. "Well, just so long as Stanley doesn't pick up any of her mad habits. What do you think, Stan?"

"I think your pants are burning!" said Stanley.

2

The next day, everyone got up early. Stanley put on his old school uniform, combed his hair and hurried down the stairs.

After breakfast, Stanley's mum dropped Stanley and his dad at the train station on her way to work.

"Dad will travel with you to Rutting Town and I'll see you in a couple of weeks. Don't forget to give Aunt Mabel a kiss for me!" said Mum.

....

It was early afternoon by the time the train arrived in Rutting Town. Aunt Mabel was waiting for them on the platform.

"My, how you've grown, Stanley," she said as he got off the train.

Stanley felt uneasy. His aunt seemed to look straight through him with her wide, googly eyes.

"She looks so crispy and frazzled," he thought.

Just then, a train arrived at the opposite platform. It was the train that would take Stanley's dad home again.

"Good to see you again, Mabel," Dad said nervously.

Then Dad turned to Stanley and said, "Good luck, son. We'll come up and see you in a couple of weeks. And when we do, we expect to hear great things."

"Okay," said Stanley. "I'm sure I'll make lots of new friends."

"Make sure they're the kind who help you with your studies," said Dad, wagging his finger. "And do everything the teachers tell you."

"I will," said Stanley.

"You look ... different, Aunty," said
Stanley after his dad had gone. "I thought
you had brown hair." Aunt Mabel's few
remaining hairs stuck up like burnt
matchsticks. In fact, everything she wore
looked burnt. He remembered what his
mum had said and he gave her a quick
kiss on the cheek.

RUTTING TOWN

"Brrr," he shivered. "You are cold, Aunty."

"I'm afraid it's a bit draughty on the school bus," she smiled. Aunt Mabel pointed to a burnt-out wreck parked outside the train station. A lot of other people were staring at it too. All the windows were blown out, the tyres were melted and the bonnet was badly dented.

13

"What happened?" Stanley exclaimed.

"I had a bit of a bump," his aunt replied. "But don't worry. We have a new driver now."

Behind the black curtains in the bus windows, Stanley saw a hundred pairs of eyes staring right at him. The strange thing was, he couldn't see the faces they belonged to.

Aunt Mabel grabbed Stanley's bag. "Let's hurry up and get on. We don't want to keep your school chums waiting," she said. "They should have been in bed hours ago."

"But it's the middle of the day," thought Stanley.

15

3

Stanley got on the bus. As soon as he saw the driver, he screamed.

The children on the bus started to laugh. Stanley was cross. "Why do people only notice me when there's something to laugh at?" he thought.

"Stanley, this is Rameses," his aunt explained. Stanley stared at the mummy behind the wheel and started to shake. The mummy grinned and waved.

"Now Stanley, it's rude to stare," his aunt scolded, moving him on. "Rameses is very sensitive." Then she put her face close to Stanley's ear and whispered, "He's Egyptian. They say his tomb was amazing. It's a shame they had to dig him up really."

It was hard to see anything on the dark bus, but Stanley thought the children near the front looked as white as ghosts. They also looked as if they hadn't washed or combed their hair for years and years.

"New boy, new boy," chanted the rowdy children. Stanley thought his aunt might ask them to calm down. But she didn't.

Aunt Mabel got Stanley to his seat just in time. Rameses grunted and started the engine. With a big bang and a burst of black smoke, the bus started its journey. Rameses drove so fast that the buildings of Rutting Town were just a blur to Stanley. They were soon driving through wild, open countryside.

"Rutland Moor," his aunt shouted over the growl of the engine. "Isn't it lovely?"

"I can't see anything but grass, bushes and rocks," Stanley shouted back.

"How far is it to the nearest toy shop?" Stanley asked. He wanted to buy a new computer game with some money his dad had given him on the train.

"Shops?" laughed his aunt. "There's nothing but sheep and wolves for miles!"

Just then, a hand tapped Stanley on the shoulder. He turned around. There was no one there. Then the hand tapped him on the other shoulder. Stanley jumped in fright.

"Aaaargh!" he cried as the floating hand pinched his nose and ran off. The children on the bus were roaring with laughter.

"I've got my eye on you," growled a scary voice from the back.

Stanley turned around again and peered into the darkness.

To his horror, a tough-looking girl with one eye was staring right at him.

"I said, I've got my eye on you," she repeated.

Aunt Mabel poked Stanley in the ribs.

"It's on top of your head, love," she pointed out.

Stanley felt something slimy trickling down the back of his neck.

"Eeeuurgh!" he shrieked, brushing it quickly to the floor. The slippery eye gave him a cheeky wink.

"Aaaargh!" screamed Stanley.

It was late afternoon when they reached
Rutland Hall.

"Wow!" Stanley cried when he saw it.

The children on the bus were fighting to get off.

"Off to bed, it's late," his aunt shouted. The children flew out of the bus windows and straight through the front wall of the mansion.

"What school is this?" gasped Stanley.

His aunt smiled playfully. "Welcome to Ghoul School, Stanley," she replied.

Thick clouds of smoke rose from her ears. "Come on, I'll take you to your room," Aunt Mabel said.

Aunt Mabel led Stanley to the great front doors and opened them with a large, rusty key. They creaked open. Flickering candles cast long shadows across the stone floor of the hall.

"It's so quiet and cold," Stanley whispered, shivering.

The hall was like the big Egyptian room at the British Museum. Everywhere Stanley looked there was an ancient coffin inside a glass case. Some of them even had mummies inside. Aunt Mabel hurried Stanley up the staircase.

"We need to get you to bed," she told him. "Tomorrow's a big day."

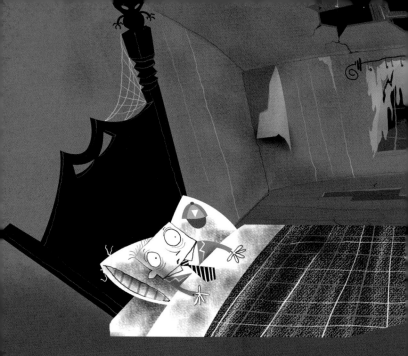

At the end of a long corridor, Aunt Mabel opened the door to Stanley's bedroom. There was nothing in it except a large four-poster bed covered in dust and cobwebs. Feeling tired after the long journey, he climbed in.

"You'll have a great view of the stars later," said his aunt, pointing to the roof.

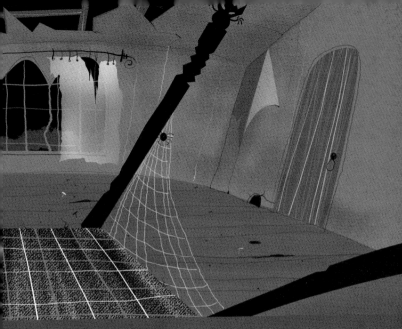

Stanley gazed up through the big hole. The sky was already turning red.

"Are you sure I'm going to fit in here, Aunty?" he yawned.

"I hope so, Stanley," said his aunt. "I told your mum we would unlock your hidden talents."

Stanley had no idea what these hidden talents might be.

5

"Breakfast!" called Aunt Mabel, walking in with a beaker of red juice and a big plate of toast and jam.

"But it's the middle of the night!" exclaimed Stanley, sitting up. He was still in his school uniform.

"Exactly," said his aunt. "School-time."

Everything seemed a bit topsy-turvy to Stanley, but he didn't like to say.

Aunt Mabel sat on the edge of the bed while he gobbled the toast and drank the juice.

"Thanks, Aunty," he smiled. "What was the drink?"

"Beetle juice," she replied.

Stanley gulped. "And the jam?"

"Toadstool."

"Oh," said Stanley, a little surprised. "I thought it all tasted a bit ... different."

But Stanley did feel refreshed, so he got out of bed and reached for his comb.

"I had better smarten myself up a bit," he said.

Aunt Mabel put the comb to one side and messed up his hair. "So much to learn and so little time," she sighed.

Aunt Mabel took Stanley by the hand and led him downstairs. "How about we sit in on a few lessons?" she asked. "Let's start with PE with Mrs Gangoul."

"Fine," said Stanley.

Stanley joined the class under a full moon on the tennis courts outside. Mrs Gangoul was wearing her tennis whites. In fact, everything about Mrs Gangoul was white and ghostly.

"Excellent," cheered Aunt Mabel. "Eye-ball tennis!"

None of the children were playing very nicely.

"Cheat!" "What a rubbish shot!" "Out!" "No it wasn't!" The noise was unbearable.

"I can't do this!" Stanley cried.

Everyone stopped.

"That's the new boy," yelled a wild-looking girl. "He looks a bit of a wimp."

Stanley felt upset, but was too polite to say. Mrs Gangoul just ignored him.

"She's just like horrid Mr Tinker at my old school," he thought. Stanley was starting to feel a bit twisted-up inside.

Next, Aunt Mabel took Stanley to an arm-wrestling lesson with Professor Riptorman. The pupils started to make fun of Stanley when he tried to join in.

"He's not a ghoul," shouted one of the boys.

"Yeah, but he looks dead," said another.

The children laughed wildly. The knot inside Stanley's stomach was getting tighter by the hour.

6

The next two weeks passed very quickly. While Aunt Mabel was busy in the school kitchen, Stanley tried his best to fit in.

The other pupils teased him at first. "What are you good at?" they would sneer. But by the end of the first week, they just ignored him. It was as if he wasn't even there. Stanley found this even worse.

"It's just like my last school," he told his aunt.

"Don't worry," she replied. "When Mrs Tanglefoot unlocks your hidden talents, then they'll take notice."

His aunt's words were kind, but Stanley was feeling more and more upset – and angry!

The history lessons about ancient Egypt were Stanley's favourite. Professor Zigoul taught him how to unravel a mummy and pickle a daddy.

Then there were lessons on waking up
zombies with Professor Morgue, and
putting a skeleton back together with
Mrs Ichingbone. But the lesson all the
ghouls talked about was Frightology,
with the headteacher, Mrs Tanglefoot.

"Yeah," said Max Goblack,
"Frightology's the best!"

Max was a short ghoul
with bow-legs and
strange pointy ears.
He was Stanley's
only friend.

FRIGHTOLOGY

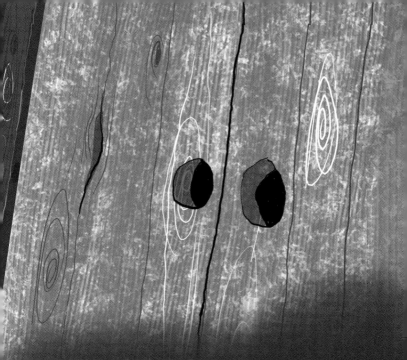

At the end of the first two weeks, Stanley had his first lesson in Frightology. The whole school was a buzz of excitement. Stanley had heard so much about Mrs Tanglefoot, but he had never seen her.

"Whatever you do, don't draw attention to yourself," Max warned.

When all the pupils and teachers were in the hall, the dinner mummies locked and bolted the doors. There was a deathly hush. Then, Stanley heard knocking knees and chattering teeth.

"Everyone seems a bit ... scared," he whispered to Max.

Just then, there was a loud, spooky howl. Ghouls everywhere looked uneasy as the room slowly filled with an ice-cold mist.

"Someone's talking," hissed a spooky, faceless voice.

A blizzard exploded into the room. The ghouls covered their ears.

"Is that Mrs Tanglefoot?" Stanley asked Max, a bit too loudly.

Stanley looked up with terror at the phantom headteacher.

Mrs Tanglefoot's long gown and white hair were flapping wildly in the snowstorm.

"She must be the size of a double-decker bus," Stanley trembled. And then he realised. The phantom headteacher was staring straight at him.

"Now you're in trouble," Max quivered.

"Come here!" Mrs Tanglefoot yelled.

7

The blizzard stopped. Stanley got up and walked nervously up onto the stage. Mrs Tanglefoot lowered her glasses and peered down at him.

"Someone tell this boy why we're all here!" she shouted.

"To study Frightology, Miss. So we can be the scariest ghouls ever!" replied the tough-looking girl with the wandering eye. Stanley remembered her from the bus and shivered.

"Excellent, Mildred," said Mrs Tanglefoot smiling.

Stanley gazed into the ghoul school crowd. "They're going to throw me to the zombies when they find out I'm not a real ghoul," he thought.

"Your aunt thinks you have hidden talents," said Mrs Tanglefoot with a grin. "But we don't!"

She bent down to peer into Stanley's eyes. "Scare me!" she demanded. "We're in a haunted mansion. Do something that makes me jump! Or shall I do something to scare *you*?"

Mrs Tanglefoot grinned again and the crowd gasped.

"She'll scare him out of his wits!" Stanley heard someone whisper.

He started to shake. He liked drama, but Mrs Tanglefoot was scary. Stanley closed his eyes and imagined he was a zombie.

He stiffened his arms and legs and waddled towards her. "I'm coming to get you!" he roared. Everyone laughed wildly.

"Rubbish!" Mrs Tanglefoot cried.

Stanley made a face. "How rude!" he thought. He was starting to feel angry.

"Imagine you're a monster," she told him. "A monster which can stand up for itself and that everyone notices."

Stanley screwed his eyes tightly shut. He gritted his teeth and remembered how horrible it was to be ignored all the time. It didn't take long for his anger to boil. He imagined himself as a huge, fearsome monster with wild hair and fiery eyes.

"Come on, Stanley!" cried Aunt Mabel from the back of the hall.

Stanley's body jerked. Again the crowd gasped.

"He's growing!" cried his aunt with glee.

Stanley imagined his monster with huge arms that could crash through walls.

"Watch out!" someone cried. "His arms are going crazy."

Stanley could feel his body becoming more powerful and hairy by the second. He opened his eyes.

Ghouls and zombies everywhere were running for cover. "Help!" they cried. Stanley was so big now that his head was breaking through the roof.

"Excellent!" cried Mrs Tanglefoot.

Stanley saw Mrs Gangoul shivering behind a chair. He picked her up and hung her by her tennis shoes from the roof.

"Get me down at once!" she cried.

"She'll remember me now," Stanley thought.

8

Stanley's parents had driven half the night to get to Rutland Hall.

"I didn't realise it was so far," said Mum as she turned the car onto the drive.

"And spooky," said Dad.

"Well, let's hope Stanley's got a bit more spirit and discovered a special talent for something," said Mum.

Suddenly, there was an explosion. For a second Mum thought she saw a monster's head blasting up through the roof.

"It's the school!" cried Dad. "It's caving in. I thought you said they were restoring it, not knocking it down!"

"There's Aunt Mabel," cried Mum, peering through the haze. "What has she done to her hair?"

Aunt Mabel ran up to the car. "It's Stanley," she shouted. "He's causing absolute chaos!"

Towering up through the roof, Stanley saw his parents' car. "They had better not see me like this!" he thought.

Stanley's body began to shrink, and a minute later he ran out to greet his parents.

"Stanley!" cried his dad, staring at Stanley's grubby, un-ironed shirt. "You're such ... a mess!"

"Oh, Mabel. I'm so sorry," sobbed Mum.

"Sorry?" exclaimed his aunt, "But Stanley has found his hidden talent!"